Minnie and Moo

and the
Musk of Zorro

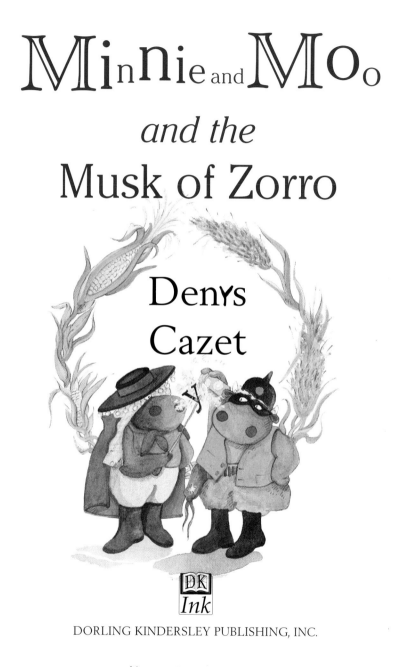

Denys Cazet

DK
Ink

DORLING KINDERSLEY PUBLISHING, INC.

To Rick Masar, for having shared
the consequences of Sister Borgia's yardstick

Dorling Kindersley Publishing, Inc., 95 Madison Avenue, New York, New York 10016
Visit us on the World Wide Web at http://www.dk.com
Text and illustrations copyright © 2000 by Denys Cazet

Library of Congress Cataloging-in-Publication Data
Cazet, Denys.
Minnie and Moo and the musk of Zorro / by Denys Cazet. — 1st ed.
p. cm.
"A DK Ink book."
Summary: Cows Minnie and Moo masquerade as the hero Zorro in order
to protect the barnyard, but the results are not quite what they intended.
ISBN 0-7894-2652-8 (hc)   ISBN 0-7894-2653-6 (pb)
[1. Cows—Fiction. 2. Chickens—Fiction. 3. Heroes—Fiction.]
I. Title PZ7.C2985Me2000 [E]—dc21 00-021280

The illustrations for this book were created with pencil and watercolor.
The illustration on these pages was drawn in pencil.
The text of this book is set in 18 point Berling.
Printed and bound in U.S.A.
First edition, 2000
2 4 6 8 10 9 7 5 3 1

Who?

The late summer sun warmed the hill.

Minnie snored softly.

Moo put her book down and sighed.

She looked at the world

beyond the farm.

"Where have they all gone?"

she said sadly.

"Who?" Minnie snorted.

"The good guys," said Moo.

"Heroes!"

Minnie opened one eye.

"Who?"

Moo held up her book.

"Zorro!" she said.

Minnie sat up.

She pointed at the book.

"You have been reading, haven't you?"

Moo hid the book behind her back.

"And thinking, too!" Minnie added.

"It was just a small think,"
said Moo, shrugging.

"Double trouble!" said Minnie.

"But Minnie! Think about it!"

"Too busy," said Minnie.

Moo raised her arms to the sky.

"What do we really *give* to the world?"

"About a gallon a day," said Minnie.

"Oh, Minnie. I don't mean milk.

I mean . . . helping others.

You know. Doing good deeds."

"Getting hooked up

to an electric milker

is a good deed," said Minnie.

"What else is there, Moo?"

"This, Minnie. It's full of heroes."

Moo held up her book.

"The Musk of Zorro!"

Who Are We?

Moo leaned against the old oak tree
and wondered.
Was Minnie right?
Are we all just cows
waiting to get hooked up
to the electric milker?
Are we all just . . .

"Maybe you are right, Moo,"

said Minnie.

She put her arm around Moo.

"Oh, Minnie," said Moo.

"I think I think too much."

"That's okay," said Minnie.

"I eat too much."

Moo smiled.

"Who was 'Zorro'?" Minnie asked.

"A famous bull," said Moo.

"I see," said Minnie. "A hero?"

Moo nodded.

"Yes," she said. "Most days

he just hung around.

But on some days,

he dressed in black and scared away

the bad guys with a sword."

"How?" Minnie asked.

"Zip! Zap! Zip!" said Moo.

"He marked their shirts with the letter Z."

"I'll bet *that* scared them," said Minnie.

"That, and the smell," said Moo.

"The musk of Zorro

put fear in their hearts."

Dolores and Juanita

Minnie looked at Zorro's picture.

"I've seen these clothes before."

"Where?"

"In the old trunk in the barn—"

Moo gasped.

She grabbed Minnie's arm.

"This is our chance," she said.

"Moo, what are you talking about?"

"Heroes," said Moo.

"What?"

"Minnie," said Moo. "Think about it.
All we need are the clothes, a sword—"

"—the musk," Minnie added.

"Moo, you are not going to find
the musk of Zorro lying around
in a spray can!"

"Minnie, we could be heroes.

I will be called by my Spanish name,

Juanita del Zorro del Moo.

You will be my faithful friend

Dolores del Zorro del Minnie."

"Moo, listen to me—"

"Listen to the world," said Moo.

"It cries out for heroes!"

Moo turned and ran toward the barn.

"Follow me, Dolores," she called.

Minnie sighed.

She threw up her arms.

"Juanita!" she shouted.

"Wait for me!"

The One-Eyed Mask

Minnie brushed the hay off the trunk.

"This one!" she said, opening it up.

She pulled out a pair of pants

and a pair of black boots.

"And here's a cape and a hat," she said.

"Here's something for you," Moo said.

"A mask, fat pants, and a helmet."

"Thank you," said Minnie.

"Look, Minnie! A sword!
We can tape this lipstick
to the end of it . . . see!
Zip! Zap! Zip!"

18

"You need a mask," said Minnie.

They looked and looked.

They couldn't find a mask for Moo.

"What about this?" said Minnie.

She held up a shirt

with a hole in it.

Moo put the shirt over her head.

She peeked out of the hole.

"Can you see?" Minnie asked.

"Yes," said Moo.

"LOOK!"

Minnie took a spray can
out of the trunk.

"Oh, Minnie," said Moo.

"Could it be?" Minnie asked.

Moo looked at the can.

"What does it say?" asked Minnie.

"Hmm," muttered Moo,

"something about armpits."

Minnie pushed the spray button.

The can hissed

and filled the air with a sweet smell.

"The musk of Zorro!" Minnie gasped.

Heroes

Juanita del Zorro del Moo
and Dolores del Zorro del Minnie
opened the gate and crept in.
The chickens stared at them.
Minnie stared at the chickens.
"Why are they looking at us?"
"They are only chickens," said Moo.

"They don't understand
that we have come to save them
from the fox."
"Don't they know a hero
when they see one?" Minnie said.

The chickens moved
into the corner of the yard.

Minnie and Moo hid behind the door.

They waited and waited.

"Listen," said Moo. "Someone

just came into the chicken yard."

"The fox!" Minnie whispered.

Outside, the rooster

strutted into the yard.

"Hi, girls," he said. "Sorry I'm late!"

Suddenly, out jumped

Juanita del Zorro del Moo.

Out jumped

Dolores del Zorro del Minnie.

Zip, zap, zip

went the sword of Zorro!

"Musk the fox," shouted Moo.

Sssst, sssst, sssst

went the musk of Zorro!

Minnie stopped.

She looked around.

"Good job!" Moo said.

"You scared him off!"

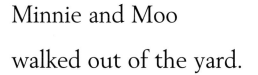

Minnie and Moo

walked out of the yard.

The rooster waved the smell away.

He looked at the letter Z on his chest.

He looked at the chickens.

"Geez," he said. "I said I was sorry."

The Bad Guys

Juanita del Zorro del Moo

and Dolores del Zorro del Minnie

crept up to the farmer's house.

"There," said Moo.

"Do you see them?"

Two shadows moved about in the yard.

"Bad guys," said Minnie.

"It's hero time!" said Moo.

"I'm ready," said Minnie.

"NOW!" shouted Moo.

They rushed the two shadows.

Zip, zap, zip

went the sword of Zorro.

Sssst, sssst, sssst

went the musk of Zorro.

Minnie leaped
into the air.

She landed on both of them.

She rolled over them twice.

They didn't move.

"Gosh," said Moo.

"They're flatter than a pancake!"

"Don't mess with Dolores,"

Minnie puffed.

The Farmer's Underwear

The porch light went on.

"Hide!" said Moo.

Minnie and Moo hid behind the bushes.

The farmer stepped out onto the porch.

"Where?" he said. "I don't see them."

The farmer's wife came out.

"On the clothesline," she said.

"Where else would I hang

your long underwear to dry?"

"Well, they're gone," said the farmer.

"What's that awful smell—skunk?"

The farmer's wife

looked at the clothesline.

She looked down.

"There," she said.

"The wind must have blown them off."

She picked up the underwear.

"Goodness!" she said. "Look!

Someone wrote a *U* on this one

and a *P* on that one!"

"Why would anyone write 'UP,'

in lipstick, on your underwear?"

"How would I know?" said the farmer.

"Hmm," said the farmer's wife.

"Coral pink lipstick and . . .

they're backward!"

"What?" said the farmer.

"Your underwear!

This pair was over here.

Now read it!"

"P . . . U . . . !" said the farmer.

"Someone wrote 'P U' on my underwear?"

The farmer's wife

put her hands on her hips.

"And I know exactly who

wears coral pink!"

She pointed at the bushes.

"You won't get away with this,

Elsie Maxwell!"

8

The Heroes Go Home

The farmer's wife wagged her finger.

"I know you did this, Elsie!"

"Mildred," said the farmer,

"Elsie Maxwell lives a mile away."

"She also wears coral pink lipstick.

Nobody wears

coral pink anymore," said Mildred.

"I think it's those two cows on the hill,"
said the farmer.

"John, you're being silly.
Elsie Maxwell is still mad at me
for winning the blue ribbon
at the fair last year!"

The farmer and his wife
walked back to the house.

"Mildred, if Elsie is mad at *you*,
why didn't she write
on *your* underwear?"

Mildred went into the house.

"I'm going to call Elsie
and give her a piece of my mind!"

The farmer looked around the yard.

"I think it's those cows," he muttered.

He closed the door

and turned off the porch light.

Minnie and Moo hurried up the hill.

They sat down under the old oak tree.

Moo yawned.

Minnie stretched.

A light went on at the Maxwell house.

After a few minutes,
Minnie leaned back
and closed her eyes.
Moo took out her new book.
Minnie opened her eyes
and looked at Moo.
"I knew it!" she said. "Reading again!"
"Oh," said Moo. "I . . ."
Minnie smiled
and closed her eyes again.
"Read to me," she said.

"Really?" said Moo.

"Really," said Minnie.

Moo opened her new book.

Moo began:

"The first Monday of the month

of April 1626 . . ."